THE FACES

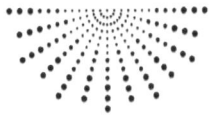

DOUGLAS CLEGG

ALKEMARA
PRESS

For Raul

STAND-ALONE NOVELS

Afterlife

Breeder

The Children's Hour

Dark of the Eye

Goat Dance

The Halloween Man

The Hour Before Dark

Mr. Darkness

Naomi

Neverland

You Come When I Call You

NOVELLAS & SHORT NOVELS

The Attraction

The Dark Game (Two Novelettes)

Dinner with the Cannibal Sisters

Isis

The Necromancer

Purity

The Words

SERIES

THE HARROW SERIES

Nightmare House, Book 1

Mischief, Book 2

The Infinite, Book 3

The Abandoned, Book 4

The Necromancer

Isis

THE CRIMINALLY INSANE SERIES

Bad Karma, Book 1

Red Angel, Book 2

Night Cage, Book 3

THE VAMPYRICON TRILOGY

The Priest of Blood, Book 1

The Lady of Serpents, Book 2

The Queen of Wolves, Book 3

THE CHRONICLES OF MORDRED

Mordred, Bastard Son

COLLECTIONS

Lights Out: Collected Stories

Night Asylum

The Nightmare Chronicles

Wild Things

The Poisoner's Garden & Others

BOX SET BUNDLES

Bad Places (3 Novels)

Coming of Age (3 Dark Novellas)

Dark Rooms (3 Novels)

Criminally Insane: The Series (3 Novels)

Halloween Chillers

Harrow: Three Novels (Books 1-3)

Harrow: Four Novels (Books 1-4)

Haunts (8 Novel Box Set)

Lights Out (3 Collection Box Set)

Night Towns (3 Novels)

The Vampyricon Trilogy (3 Novels)

GET DOUGLAS CLEGG'S
NEWSLETTER

Get book updates, price drop news flashes, and exclusive offers—become a V.I.P. member of Douglas Clegg's long-running email newsletter:

http://DouglasClegg.com/newsletter

CONTENTS

THE FACES

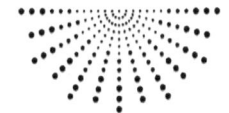

"He was there or was not there: not there if I didn't see him."

— HENRY JAMES, FROM *TURN OF THE SCREW*

THE STORE OF LAST CHANCE

"Fills me with absolute dread—this whole Friday night business," came a substantial baritone.

The voice held its own amidst an unexpected quiet that arose within the chaotic clinking of cups and locust chatter of the after-work crowd on a peculiarly warm and breezy October evening, not quite dark.

If you sat nearby you might notice the man who spoke these words—dressed in the forgettable office attire of the moment, hair smoothed back from ears, uncomfortable look on face.

"Harold, come *on. Dread?*" The woman across the table didn't even glance up from her newspaper.

Harold checked the dark depths of his coffee cup then moved up to her face, past shoulders, to the man sitting at the next table behind theirs.

"You know I'm no good at small talk, Margaret," Harold said.

Margaret looked out the window onto the street as someone handsome passed by unaware. Her gaze returned briefly to Harold before settling back to the papers.

"*Everything* we talk about is 'small talk,'" she said. "You're being *ridiculous.*"

"So I've heard." He took one last sip from his cup before setting it down. "People pretend too much as it is at those things. They ask questions but don't wait for answers. It's irritating."

"That's called being *social.* It's a *party.* It's *fun.* It's getting *out.* It's free *drinks.*" She reached across the table to pat his hand as if he were a big baby.

One could not help but feel that she did all this by rote, as if this woman could comfort him in her sleep, an old habit, a go-to, even a tic.

Margaret mentioned a "terrible story" from the papers, "someone got attacked four blocks from here, over by the old warehouse" and then "look, you're going whether you like it or not," and "I can't wait to see what Roger wears, he's always good with costumes," all of this nearly in the same breath.

Harold made a back-of-throat grumble. "I hate that the sun goes down so early this time of year. I wasted the entire summer."

"It *definitely* gets dark too soon—what time is

it?" Margaret checked her watch. "We should scoot."

She turned and signaled for the bill.

"How do I look?" she said.

"Same as three minutes ago."

"My eyeliner usually needs a pick-me-up about now."

"You look fine, Margaret," he said. "Fresh as a daisy, Daisy."

"I'm nobody's Daisy."

Roughly the same age as Harold, Margaret had a white streak through thick black hair chopped short. She wore a wildly oversized cable-knit sweater with a string of pearls hanging down from her neck.

Harold again looked over her shoulder to the table beyond.

"Something in my hair?" Margaret asked.

"Huh?"

"You keep looking back there."

"I really think we're being observed," Harold whispered.

"By the famous 'him'?"

"Told you not to look."

"You did *not*," Margaret said. "Nobody cares enough to watch the two of us, believe me."

"He's always just *there*."

"Maybe he knows you from somewhere."

She glanced behind her chair in that way one might when pretending *not* to look.

Harold *had* wondered if this might be a forgotten classmate from college or even someone seen in a crowd downtown.

He rarely forgot a name or face but couldn't place this one at all—outside of having seen the guy once or twice before at this particular café.

Yet he recognized something subliminally familiar about him.

Perhaps someone of note?

Politician? Local celebrity? A face from a morning news show?

Perhaps his face was just an ordinary one. Nothing remarkable about it other than overall blandness, even with his very slight smile.

Not unpleasant.

Perhaps he's not even eavesdropping. May just be sitting there lost in thought.

Harold would've examined the stranger's face a bit longer, but Margaret tugged him back to their purpose.

"Look, we've got maybe forty minutes before everything closes."

It was her turn to pay the check. She muttered about poor service and not getting that promised third refill.

"Let's just skip it," he said.

"Skip out on the tip?"

"No, I mean this whole thing. We can go to a movie or something instead."

"You'd never go anywhere you're supposed to if I wasn't around," Margaret said.

Minutes later, she nudged Harold along the sidewalk toward a series of shops just at the turn in the road.

"Imagine." He glanced up and down the block. "An entire street of stores selling other people's trash."

"Isn't it *great*? We could find all *kinds* of stuff. *Look* at the Halloween displays! You could go as a cowboy—or a *clown*."

"Weirdo I may be, but I don't need to highlight it with a big red nose."

She led him beyond his inclinations in and out of shops with names like "Yesterday's Treasures," "This 'N' That," and "What-Nots."

"Parties are social gallows," he said as they strolled up and down aisles.

Out one door, in through another.

At the fifth shop, he said, "Where are we—some moldy version of secondhand hell?"

The big front window displayed a large carousel horse, splintery and paint-peeled, beside a rusted pig weathervane. Margaret—first to open the shop door

—continued her many-storied concept for a successful blueprint of the next few months "when you need to finally figure everything out."

"Quit matronizing me," he repeated an old joke between them. She *was* mothery and smothery, taking him shopping for the right clothes and over-seeing his haircuts and how he should organize his routine.

Only now, he appreciated it less than during their college years.

Hypnotized once again by the hum of her chatter as she pulled possible suits and jackets and checker-board trousers out from various racks, Harold felt trapped inside the store of last chance at ten minutes to closing.

He swore inside himself—where no one else was allowed—that it would be the last trash dump he'd ever enter in his life.

He followed her down narrow and somewhat smelly aisles of dead people's flotsam, winding around and among musty rows of rags and patches hanging beneath a long series of windows at the back.

She drew several coats out and held each one up in turn for his approval. "This could be your prom costume. Or maybe a butler. You'd make a great butler."

She's distracting me, he thought. *I'm being railroaded into this.*

Finally, she pulled out four unusual, somewhat dated suit jackets and mismatched slacks. She piled them on a chair.

"None of those are my size," he said. "And they're ugly."

"They are not. You'd look nice in this."

"Someone may have died in that," he said. "You smell what I smell? What if someone sweated in them...or worse?"

Eventually, weary of her pushiness and tired of banter, he blindly reached into the long rows of twisted hangers and pulled out a bitter plum: a wacky costume that must have been ordinary in its time.

"Stinks like a steamy plate of 1956 with a side of rotting magnolias," he said.

"Mid-century modern and seersucker. Not bad. The dry cleaners can spruce it up. What will you be? 1950s man? Do we need to find a straw hat? We need a mask to make it truly a costume. Want to be a werewolf in seersucker?"

"I'll suffocate. How about just going with *my* face? I can contort it. Or wear a monocle."

"Don't be silly. You can't go as 'you.' The point of a costume party is you're *not* 'you.' You need a new look."

"Can't we find one of those jaunty half-masks so I can be a man of mystery? I'm not going to be something uglier than I already am."

"Pull up your big boy pants for once," she said. "Sometimes I wonder how you've made it this far in life."

This comment, obnoxious yet innocent, spoken light as air, a sweet grin on her face, a sly touch on the shoulder so he'd know she meant it in fun and not as a serious notion, had come at the wrong moment in his life.

Harold hadn't told her about the night before, the three o'clockness of the morning, that growling loathsomeness he felt on such nights, the staring at a fat little bottle of pills and a tall slim bottle of bad whiskey beside yet another bottle brimming with the amber liquid codeine prescribed when he'd had a terrible cough that kept him from sleeping. Nor did he mention the cooling bathtub he'd sat beside in his apartment's tiny bathroom after a night of wandering alleys and past memories; the weeping and bawling like a baby; his face collapsing as he saw his pitiful self in the mirror.

And then there were the hundreds of thoughts running around in his brain, all of them emptying into avenues that led to one dreadful cul-de-sac.

He never told anyone about those nights.

A party, he thought as he stood beside her and looked at the wall of masks.

Planning for a party with a buddy, and no one would know about the things that three o'clock could do to you.

Quickly scrubbing his memory until he remained in the here and now, which happened to be inside the junk shop at nearly six in the evening, Harold began searching in earnest for a helmet, some solid face armor and—for the moment—he gave in to the wisdom of Margaret.

Strange to feel one way during those mid-dark-to-mid-light hours and now, in late afternoon, imagine dressing up by hiding one's face from the world.

After a minute, he noticed a particular rubber mask hanging among several of its lesser brethren (demons, clowns, witches, ghouls) on the wall by the sign marked "Fun Party Ideas."

The mask caught his eye because it was not an unfamiliar one.

"*The Faces*," he said, recognizing and naming the family from which this particular face was born.

"You don't think *that's* too ridiculous?" Margaret barely gave his choice a sidelong glance.

She obviously didn't understand *The Faces*.

Well, of course, she wouldn't have read the Sunday funnies as a kid. Their generation rarely did. It was from his father's time, mostly. And his father, something of a hoarder who kept every single memento of his childhood, now dead six years, had loved that comic strip above all others.

Harold didn't think the rubbery visage ridiculous at all, nor did he even listen to her arguments against this rather bland mask with its placid facial expression.

The face before him made him smile. Reminded him of happy parts of his childhood. *The piles of old Sunday papers Dad collected to be later turned into hats and forts and ships. His dad's joy at showing him his scrapbooks of favorite comic strips cut out when he'd been a boy.*

Margaret tried to discourage him by finding a mask of a devil and then one that looked like a recent president, but this only fanned his devotion to the one he'd picked.

The unrelenting pleasantness of this particular face appealed to him. It was not too handsome, not too perfect, just off but so slightly it made him happy for reasons of nostalgia if nothing else.

The strong dimpled chin, the gently smiling lips, the perfect eyebrows, the way the ears slightly stuck out—all added a layer of near-imperceptible vulnerability and appeal.

Won't have to be myself for one night.

The evening of the party, he went to pick her up.

2

SOCIAL BUTTERFLY

Not precisely a date (they were never dates, though there was a drunken fumble sophomore year in college which ended in unbuttoned shirts, unzipped things, and a bit of embarrassment but nothing further than a laugh and a second bottle of cheap wine), Harold took the role of escort for her as a way to not feel so alone in his tiny apartment.

Margaret showed up dressed as shabby Marie Antoinette. "Post-guillotine," Margaret told anyone who would ask.

The wig looked sloppy, which suited her fine. The spiraling cotton candy concoction was too heavy to wear and made her scalp itch anyway. She'd come up with the joke of being Antoinette carrying her own head.

She didn't take the illusion very far because her

head was clearly visible on her shoulders, her face completely powdered so that her noticeable nose entirely vanished above bright cherry red lips inset as a valentine kiss with a too-large beauty mark that Harold kept calling "your wandering mole," once he'd seen it.

"No fair," he told her. "You're not wearing a mask."

"I tried. It *stank*. Like *vomit*. I'd have been sick *all* night if I'd worn that *thing*."

He didn't slip his own mask on until they rang the doorbell at a house belonging to someone named Roger Lewis whom Harold barely knew, a slightly older acquaintance from college, too successful and—like Margaret—a product of the Engineering school and not from Humanities, where Harold had studied literature and (he felt) bullshit.

Once inside the successful Mr. Lewis's home, after meeting the wife (Avery, in a ballerina outfit) and the wife's best friend (Judy Something, dressed as a sexy pirate), Harold found it quite easy to leave the mask on.

The Faces mask felt surprisingly breathable. It fit him perfectly, unlike all those masks he'd worn on Halloween in childhood.

Must be the new tech and breathable latex or something that makes them conform so well, he thought. *Thin, perfectly molded skin.*

He could see through the eye holes as well as he usually did, while his lips pushed into the indentations precisely where the character's lips began so he could speak through the mouth slit without muffling his voice.

But would he join in the usual small talk?

He'd never been good at making people comfortable by asking about their day or their work or where they were planning to go for a vacation or about the "children question" (*to have or have not, brats or blessings?*) or the future dreams game (*where do you want to be in five years?*)

He didn't want to mingle much anyway after seeing a few folks there that he'd prefer to avoid.

He opted for drinking alone in a dim corner far from the madding crowd, imagining that he was, indeed, the comic strip character "Joe Face," favorite son of the Face family, smiling pleasantly while the world spun insanely around him.

He could sulk behind the mask, snarl, grimace, chuckle, weep, and all anyone would see was that mildly bemused, self-satisfied look.

Harold felt generally fine not having to be himself or to pretend he was having a nice time.

You might even feel confident, he thought.

Over that first hour of loud music and shouts of conversations, a few stragglers wandered over to chat. Some of them he'd known back in college, others were complete strangers.

After being comfortably alone with a bowl of chips and a few beers, Harold discovered that his chosen too-small sofa was the most popular piece of furniture in the room with clowns, pirates, strippers, a dollar-store princess and a pregnant angel all around, some squeezing beside him, others on the sofa's arms, and more sitting cross-legged on the floor in front of him as if he had something interesting to contribute.

A woman approached him. He guessed her costume might be that of a cocktail waitress from some past era, but he didn't want to ask and then she sprung it on him. She was dressed up as some superhero he'd never heard of—or else she'd made it up. She began to ask him about his work, his life, and then two young men brought over more beer.

One of them, dressed as a sailor, laughed like a hyena when Harold told his old standby about the priest and the frog who walk into a bar. The other one, in a get-up that seemed ill-advised (possibly a cultural misappropriation, but Harold could not tell which culture exactly among the four or five represented in the outfit) chuckled. The superhero smiled broadly and put her hand on his knee.

Someone very drunk sat nearby and kept bringing up the subjects of local crimes, arrests, the drug epidemic, and "that poor old guy whose face got smashed in behind the gas station on Willow Road out by the highway."

The conversations blended together, a mash of book talk and gossip and what was in the news and what was showing at the movie theaters around town.

A lovely seasoned lady of forty pulled a club chair close to his free knee; the sort of lady one only met in large cities, with a large inheritance and large ambitions and an impossible name. Her costume, which could only be worn by someone who no longer cared what anyone thought of them, was a gorilla outfit but with her own head at the top. Surprisingly though, this emphasized her beautiful face and deep dark eyes so that he soon became mesmerized by her anthropomorphic nonchalance.

At some point in the evening he glanced up and there was dear old Margaret, cantaloupe head with wig under her arm, her beauty spot sunk a bit on her chin, open-mouthed caught between awestruck and horrified—reminding him very much of the figure from Munch's *The Scream*.

"Well, who's the social butterfly now," she whispered when she got close enough. "Aren't you a man of hidden talents?"

Before they left for the night, someone nearby grabbed his elbow, briefly, and whispered, "I *know* you."

Clearly this stranger did not, but when Harold glanced his way it was like looking in a mirror.

"Well, we both know about *The Faces*," Harold said, chuckling. "They must've had a ton of these in the junk shops this month."

The other Joe Face then murmured something both loud enough and low enough that Harold only pieced together what he'd said a moment after, and it was either, "You can't talk here," or "you don't drink beer," or possibly, "you got to take care."

His stunt double pushed through the packed sea of the costumed and went out the front door.

Was this someone he actually knew? Someone he'd met before? The guy who'd been eavesdropping at the cafe?

That's it, Harold thought. *Has to be.*

3

A LUCKY NIGHT

"You should seriously buy a lottery ticket tonight. Or we could drive to a casino," Margaret said in the car on the way home.

"Why?"

"It's your lucky night. You were the most popular person at that party."

"Was not."

"By midnight, they were practically sitting in your lap. You could've had an orgy if you wanted to."

"If only. All anyone talked about was sophomore in college crap, either local news or D.H. Lawrence or what's on at the movies."

"Half of them were architects or engineers," she said. "They talked about what they thought you'd be interested in."

"You bribe them?"

She laughed. "You'd think so. I may have to reconfigure my opinion of you, Harry."

"Call me that again and I'll drop you at the Greyhound depot."

"I see you as Harry now," she said. "Harold is too formal. You really are more than meets the eye."

"Let's find that bus station for you."

He thought about what she'd said and wondered if he'd choose a pirate, stripper or the nun with the demon face, or the gorilla lady or the cocktail waitress in fishnet stockings or the sailor or maybe the priest with the fake erection in his trousers.

Harold wondered what it would be like making love to someone with his Joe Face mask secured at his throat and scalp.

Or to do it with someone who also wore a mask from *The Faces*.

Felt filthy to think about it, but wonderfully filthy.

A flicker of images ran through his mind of two rubber-masked people pressing their bland smiles together while orgasming.

Of course, in the car, he didn't mention this to Margaret.

Instead, he said, "I think you imagined it. They were there for the French onion dip."

"I'm not kidding, Harold. They were in your thrall."

"As Joe Face? I seriously doubt it." Then, he said, "Damn. I should've taken off the mask. I meant to."

Margaret went silent after this.

Was she mad at him? Had he said something insensitive?

When they said goodbye she wouldn't look at him and didn't even offer her usual shoulder pat.

He was so used to saying the wrong thing to people that he became paranoid that *of course* he'd said something insulting to her without realizing it.

After she left the car, he waited to see that she got inside and flicked on the light in the window on the second floor before he drove back to his place.

Once inside, he took the mask off and set the seersucker jacket on a chair.

Sitting on the edge of his bed, Harold glanced at the rubber face, now flaccid and empty, in his lap.

Joe Face, eldest son of the Face family, wore the exact same expression as the world fell apart around him. His entire family did. Yet they were getting along in the world despite the sinkholes that appeared in their driveway, despite the tornado that tore the roof off their home, the airplane crash that they all survived, their attendance at a mass funeral for victims of a forty-car pile-up on the freeway, surrounded by weeping family; but no, not the Faces.

Joe Face and his brothers (Joe-Bob, JoJo), and sisters (Jolette, Josephine, Jolene, Amy-Jo) and father (Joseph) and mother (Joanne) and uncles and aunts—even Baby Face in a stroller—all of them looked as if it was a great day for a picnic.

That was always the joke in the Sunday funny pages of his boyhood: The Faces showed the world that pleasantness no matter how grim the circumstance.

"Great day for a picnic."

That, mostly, was the extent of the strip's dialogue. A one-joke strip that had been hugely popular in his parents' generation.

But the rubber mask didn't seem funny to Harold as he pondered its expression at two in the morning.

It looked like a flayed emissary from a world he would never completely exist comfortably within, *and yet...*

Harold wished right then that he could always feel as accepted as he had during that particular costume party.

4

GREAT DAY FOR A PICNIC

"You know what'd be *delicious?*" Margaret told him at lunch a week or so after the party, gazing into his eyes with an interest that unnerved him a bit. "You should wear that costume to *work.*"

"I do look best in seersucker," he said with enough hoity-toity accent to sound ironic.

"I just mean the mask. It'd be a hoot."

"A *hoot,*" he repeated. "I'd lose my job."

"Bet you wouldn't."

"My regular-ol' face is close enough to getting the boot as it is."

"Maybe that place needs a joke. Maybe you do, too. You vastly underestimate yourself."

Harold hated his job.

Margaret knew this and hated it as much as he did "because it makes you grumpy and sour."

The job itself was tedium, absolute boredom, hours of his life wasted.

He'd never be promoted into work he really wanted to do. His twice-monthly paycheck barely covered his needs. His boss was horrible. Everyone there seemed elbowy and competitive. The mounds of spreadsheets to deal with were mind-numbing.

The only happy employee he'd met got high in the hallway bathroom twice a day, often masturbating right afterward before returning to his cubicle.

Harold had come close to quitting several times before but, later, remembering Margaret's suggestion made in jest (he assumed), he decided:

Fuck it.

He'd go to work as Joe Face, the whole nine yards, outfit from 1955 and the goony rubber mask of handsome cartoon blandness. He'd walk right into his boss's office and tell him off.

Damn the torpedoes, full speed ahead.

Sure, he'd get fired, but there might be unemployment income, which would give him several weeks to find some other job.

Worry about all that afterward.

Better to live in a box on the side of the road than work in a soul-crushing cubicle ever again.

He drank that morning.

Not usually a post-dawn drinker, Harold felt woozy after two glasses of wine. Downed some coffee.

Slapped his face for courage.

Harold got dressed in seersucker and slipped the rubber mask over his face.

There may have been one or two stares on the bus, but a gray-haired elderly lady said, out of the blue, "I feel like I know you from somewhere."

He meant to laugh and mention *The Faces*— surely she was of an age where she'd known the comic strip—but he couldn't overcome the edge of drunkenness and rancor fueling the morning's masquerade.

He pretended not to hear her.

In his building, the elevator was packed on the way up to his floor. A blonde with a stack of papers under her arm kept giving sidelong glances at him and someone behind him whispered to a co-worker, "Well, *that's* a good omen."

They get it, Harold thought.

He glanced around at them and said, "Great day for a picnic."

As he marched out onto the floor among the ant colony of cubicles, Harold noticed his boss sitting behind the glass wall of his private office.

The steam in Harold's mind seemed about to erupt as he stomped his way through the cubist labyrinth and flung open his boss's door.

"Well, sir," he said, now looming over his superior's desk, unsure of what to say next.

Will he laugh? Yell?

Harold felt nauseated.

You will be fired. You will be humiliated. Lucky to get work at a gas station after this. Or sweeping the street. You'll be evicted within a few months.

"Sit down," his boss said. "Please."

In his mind, Harold was sure this softness of tone on his boss's part meant absolute roiling fury.

"I'm fine right here," Harold said. "Standing."

Now the weird thing about Harold saying this was that on the inside, he didn't really want to say anything.

In fact, like a well-trained dog, he wanted to lie down and play dead.

But it was as if the costume had other plans for him. He wasn't Harold, he was Joe Face and Joe Face, no matter what happened in his life—whether his house got struck by lightning, his cousin John-Joseph drowned in the pool, his grandmother fell from the Empire State building on her trip to

Manhattan—would never change his bland, pleasant expression.

His father had told him the Faces were symbols of hope within the absurdity of life.

They kept on keeping on. They were unfazed by every bomb that life tossed their way.

And in this costume, Harold expressed this.

The anger inside, the fear, the trepidation, the tsunami building up from what he wanted in life versus what he got, all of it dissipated on the surface of his skin into a rather calm visage that exuded nothing but contentment and acceptance.

"Well," his boss said. "all right then. You stand. Let's talk."

After a few minutes of generally social conversation, his boss invited him to step outside for a walk. They went to sit in the nearby park on a green bench beneath the shade of a maple tree.

Harold began speaking reasonably, soberly, and not about how he actually felt but what would make his boss feel better about himself and the importance of the work they were doing, and later, over lunch, the boss started to open up about his troubles.

On the way back to the office Harold felt the touch of his boss's hand on his shoulder, a slight pat or two.

The man he'd absolutely detested before that afternoon said, "Well, I'm glad we spent this time together. I think we can come up with a solution that'll make us both happy."

Later, with Margaret, having coffee—an emergency friendship meeting—she said, "You wore it the entire time?"

Harold nodded.

Truth was, he still wore the mask at their favorite coffeehouse as he sat across from his best friend in the entire world, a woman who knew him backwards and forwards.

Before they parted that evening, she touched the edge of the rubber mask, right around the chin.

"Something's changed for the better in you."

"How so?"

"I feel like a terrible friend for saying it, but you've always been a little prickly. Just around the edges. But you've matured or something. You seem smarter. And warmer."

This bewildered him.

"I don't mean you were awful or anything. But you always seemed confused, even in school. As if you needed to find yourself. Or as if you didn't know how to talk to people in the right way. Or that no one heard you, maybe. And now, I feel like you figured it out. And I hear you. I *see* you, Harold. Maybe it's because we're getting older. Maybe it's just me. But it's like you stepped into a spotlight, right now, right this instant. You're in your prime. You need to take advantage of that."

He noticed that her eyes glistened on the edge of tears.

"I never realized what a wonderful guy you were," she said. "But I do now. And you *are*. Wonderful. Special. Remarkable."

"Let's get married," he said.

"What? Oh, ha ha. Even your jokes are better," she said.

5

A FAMILIAR FACE

When he went to brush and floss before bed that night, he glanced in the medicine cabinet mirror.

He realized that, yet again, he'd been wearing the rubber mask the entire day and night. It didn't even feel like a mask anymore.

He took the rubber skin off. Inhaled and exhaled with slow deliberation.

"I should not be doing this," he said to the mirror.

I will never wear this thing again, he told himself.

It's not me. I don't need it. I can be myself.

Harold put the mask, seersucker jacket and baggy

trousers away at the back of his closet, though he made sure they were on sturdy hangers and not just thrown around like many of his other clothes. He tried not to think about the Face family, did not spend time wondering about Margaret or her words.

She responded to the mask like everyone else seemed to be doing.

That felt wrong.

Work began to fall apart again. His boss snarled at him during a meeting. Harold felt lost in a fog within his mind half the time.

One evening, taking the bus home in midwinter, a handsome man sat across the aisle from him and at first Harold was bothered that he noticed him at all. When he looked again, the fellow seemed affable enough.

Harold even thought he might know him from somewhere, so he said, "Hey," the way he might to a buddy from school.

The man looked over at him, setting down the book he'd been reading.

"Hey there," he replied.

"I feel like I know you," Harold said without his usual hesitation of speaking in public.

"I get that a lot," the man said, and they introduced themselves with names and friendly nods.

"Maybe it was at..." and Harold ran down his past associations of schools and places and tenuous friendships, which were not that many, but Margaret was such a social butterfly she clearly might've introduced them once before.

"No," the guy said. "I'm sorry. Maybe I just have that kind of face that reminds you of someone else."

They were both silent for a moment until the man leaned over and said, "You really should put it back on, you know. Safer that way."

The man's stop came up. Before Harold could ask what he meant, the guy nodded a goodbye, "have a good one," and stepped down off the bus.

Harold held his breath as he watched him go.

For just a second, Harold became convinced that this guy—*what was his name?*—was a Face.

He flashed back to the day he and Margaret went shopping for his Halloween costume. The man in the café, perhaps? The same man at the Halloween party?

How could you identify someone from behind a mask?

That night, lying in bed after exhausting all possibilities of entertainment and distraction, Harold closed his eyes.

As he began to drift into sleep, he found himself

standing on a city street scrawled across the darkness of his closed eyelids. Entirely aware that he was slipping into dreamland but still conscious enough to scratch an itch on his hip, he was used to this transition where the dark behind his eyes turned liquid and chaotic yet calming images began to take over.

A crowd moved along at a crosswalk and one man stopped as if sensing Harold there (in this dream that remained colorless and yet with a depth of reality).

The guy turned to look directly at Harold.

As their eyes met, the stranger's face began to shift and melt into a grotesque gargoyle expression but with those staring eyes that filled Harold with tingling dread and then the whole scene froze and the face kept twisting and turning until it was an ogre face, a cartoon face of scars crisscrossing one another surrounding those widening eyes of terror.

Harold drew back from the ledge of sleep, gasping.

Opened his eyes to the dark bedroom with one tiny dot of red light from the smoke alarm on the ceiling above.

He lay there until nearly dawn, thinking about his boss and Margaret and the man on the bus, until finally he'd forgotten the moment's horror of the gargoyle face and sleep took him.

Less than a week later, despite the relative anonymity of living in a small city, Harold decided to put the mask on again.

It just seemed a smart thing to do. Nothing worked without it and what was he *supposed* to do? Just let life fall apart and return to the endless nothing of bad job, bad life, no hope?

Margaret didn't seem to notice. No one did except Harold himself and some days he was so used to the mask he even slept with it on.

Sometime in the early spring, Harold happened to see the stranger from the bus again.

At least he *thought* it was him.

6

PRESENTATION IS EVERYTHING

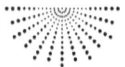

The man saw him first, actually.

During the past winter, Harold had met someone, had a fling, which ended as quickly as it began, followed by another, and another. Margaret herself flirted with him at times as if they'd only just met.

Basking in good feelings that April as afternoon turned toward evening, Harold sat on a bench overlooking the river. He'd been thinking about how this rubber mask business was really working for him in the sexual attraction arena, when he sensed someone come up behind him.

It always brought on a shiver when he felt one of them nearby; goose bumps, too, like a cold touch to the back of his neck.

Turning, he noticed that *yes, definitely another Face.*

"Mind if I sit here?"

Hesitating, Harold scooted to the side and was about to say, "I was just leaving anyway."

But he didn't leave.

There had been a few people beaten up in lonesome places around town, no one knew quite why or who had done such things. One woman had died in the attack, but it was mostly men being sent to the hospital, their faces bashed in. Harold wondered if this river park with its benches and boardwalk, empty of people close to twilight, might be one of those dangerous areas.

Should I even be here? Am I asking for trouble?

Yet, he reminded himself, *you've been in dark and lonely places elsewhere and never had a problem. Don't be paranoid.*

He sat there silently, pretending to be lost in thought and all the while feeling a pressure of urgency, an antsy squirm within.

"Your knee's trembling," the man beside him said.

Harold looked at the offending knee just as the man's hand touched it lightly as if to calm it.

"You don't need to be afraid of me," the guy said. "You're one of us now."

After a brief introduction, a bare murmur of names, this fellow (named Whit, as he introduced himself) said, "Try not to show anything much. Not here, anyway."

"You see my mask?"

"Same as you see mine," Whit said.

"I don't know why others don't see it." Even as he said these words, Harold realized that he himself hadn't completely recognized the mask when the guy on the bus wore it.

"That's easy to figure out, Harry. It's all right to call you Harry? Harold is too…well, too revealing."

"Harry's fine."

Margaret also called him Harry now and then, and so did his boss and a few co-workers. The name used to annoy him, but no more.

Whit continued. "So, about everyone else. They don't see the face because they don't really look too deeply. I mean, they see the smile, the hair, the ears. But it's not so different from pleasant faces seen in any herd. And it's all herd out there."

He paused, letting this sink in. "Well, that's a theory, but it's bandied about among our set, Harry. I'm guessing this is all new to you?"

Harry told him his own story, leaving out the three in the morning episodes and his flings during which the mask came off toward the end of the flung moment while he performed fairly embar-rassing and shameful (if pleasurable) acts.

"Well, it's difficult being us," Whit said. "Sometimes I think it would be easier to take it off and deal with what some of the unmaskers have handled. I almost envy them. But god, what they have to go through. The price of that. Why pay it?"

"But it's all sort of a joke."

"Is it, Harry? No more than any other absurdity of life. Look at the people who dye their hair blonde or bright red. Distracts from less pleasing features or even emphasizes their eyes. Some people wear makeup. Some grow beards and mustaches. Some wear hats to cover bald spots, others toupees, while there are those who shave their heads completely bald. People wear uniforms of all types to hide who they are or—at the very least—to present better versions of themselves. All those people look very much alike, and that's what we—all of us—find pleasant. Consistency of appearance. It calms the eye and relaxes the spirit. It tells us a story about them that we already accept as true. This is no different."

"Why doesn't everyone know about this?" Harold said.

"That would be the end of all of us, wouldn't it? It will never happen. People like believing what they see. Presentation is everything. Oh, they'll *say* they care about what's under the hood, but the truth is nobody cares."

"Like when someone asks, 'How you doing?'" Harold nodded. "Nobody really wants to know. They just want to hear 'fine.'"

"Or 'great day for a picnic.'"

They both chuckled.

"Say, there's a bit of a meet-up on Sunday afternoon for a bunch of us. Just cocktails and chatter. Want to come?" Before Harold could answer, Whit added, "It's really in your best interest to join in."

"How many of us…are there?"

"Well, tons. But in this part of town, maybe forty or fifty that we've figured out. I mean, it's not as if we can even recognize every one of *The Faces*. You probably missed a few just walking around this park."

"I guess so. I feel like I've met *you* several times."

"Nope," Whit said. "This is our first encounter. Doesn't need to be our last. I find your company quite…well, quite stimulating, Harry."

On Sunday, Harold showed up at the address Whit had mentioned.

7

YOU MUST BE THE NEWBIE

Harold made sure that he had the mask firmly in place before the front door opened.

A nice-looking man, big grin on his face, no mask at all, greeted him.

"Hey, I'm Bobby, you must be the newbie. Harry? Hal? Harrison? Whit's been talking about you non-stop. Oh, you can take old Joe off now. We go 'Face Naked' here. None of us need it when we gather away from prying eyes. Unless you're more comfortable with it on? Some folks are. That's okay, too."

Harold—who felt more like a Harry at the moment—followed Bobby inside.

After the get-together with a bit more information

gleaned from hanging out with his "new buddies" Whit, Bobby, Jack, the two Daves, Tom, Alex, Alice, Joan, Heather, and Debbie (the segregation of genders—though unmentioned—did not go unnoticed), Harold felt reinvigorated.

He donned the mask he now considered his Harry face and decided to go test the various theories and concepts the other Faces had debated and argued about with gusto over guacamole and martinis.

After a shared early supper out, Margaret asked him about this "mysterious party," which he'd accidentally alluded to over a third glass of wine.

"Just a bunch of bores from the office. Not much of a party, really. You know the drill: put in the required appearance, air kisses, back slaps, feigned interest, check the time and then skedaddle as soon as possible."

Harold was, of course, sworn to secrecy. Even his closest friend Margaret couldn't know about the whole Face society.

She bought his lie and began chatting about her job, how she was thinking about getting her graduate degree, then mentioned a kerfuffle with some annoying ex who kept showing up wherever she went.

The whole time Harold mentally returned to Sunday's group. All those men and women donning rubber masks on the way out. All fiercely protective of their secret society and the ideals that these comic strip characters represented for them.

He watched Margaret's face for a sign of awareness. Every time they met up, he'd check for a glimmer of recognition or perhaps a scrutinizing gaze. Would she *ever* notice the mask?

If anything, her attitude shifted in a way that didn't make him entirely uncomfortable. Margaret moved ever closer to him. Or did he only imagine it?

He'd begun to notice—in small touches, as she leaned in close to whisper minor secrets while grasping his wrist, in the sly curve of her lips—a very different Margaret than he'd known before.

Later, in the car, this was confirmed when she let her hand rest a beat too long on his lap as she reached for the seat belt, overshooting the mark entirely.

As if in scenes from some tawdry movie, she cupped his chin in her hands, which then traveled down his shirt, the top three buttons of which opened beneath her fingers. She looked at him a certain way; he felt the stirrings in an instant. How could he not?

In twenty minutes, they embraced within the powder blue walls of her apartment with its many mirrors and few chairs. They both went to the floor, digging into each other like horny feral cats—or baboons in a frenzy. All this was followed up by the expected after-moment:

Gathering clothes, drawing some of them on for unnecessary modesty, while a general feeling of sadness at the end of such pleasures overtook him.

Harold noticed that the room seemed entirely askew, its few chairs overturned and even one mirror cracked because of the exuberant athleticism of a volcanic passion.

Great day for a picnic, he thought as he did an internal postmortem on the mess they'd made around them.

Did not do as much for him as it had for her—according to the expression on her face—but the whole thing must have been, at the very least, pleasant.

As they both lay in broken pieces on itchy wool carpeting, he recalled a moment deep within the previous thirty minutes of action in which she accidentally drew off Joe Face's outer skin and—for a bare second—he noticed a kind of horror in her eyes, which widened just as he himself lengthened and pulsed.

He managed to draw that rubber mask back down without missing more than a beat.

She closed her eyes and opened them again as if she'd just swum up from the depths of a terrible dream.

Margaret never mentioned what she'd been feeling at that moment, but he knew it wasn't anything pleasurable.

He began to wonder if he'd imagined it. He wondered if *The Faces* had some hypnotic power to grant forgetfulness to those who'd peered beneath the mask.

All these new events—the mask-wearing friends who never spoke of this in public but held gatherings every so often where they'd shed masks to be themselves in moments of collective privacy and the surprising bouts of lust and rug-rolling with Margaret—became fairly frequent.

Margaret began to drop hints about the future, about where they both wanted to be in life in five or ten years, and how fun it was to have so much time alone together.

Did she suspect he had a different life when they weren't together?

Harold participated in sleazier little trysts of spontaneous combustion when someone on the street, out of nowhere, found him attractive. Of course, he knew it was Harry—or rather Joe Face—who set the honeytrap and caused that tingle, that frisson of lust, performed in animalistic ritual in cars or standing against a wall in an alley's shade or deep down in stairwells of old buildings—or any port in the storm.

Harold, or Harry, both of them, felt all of this made up for lost time in the space of less than a year.

But none of it ever cancelled out those terrible bouts of three-in-the-morning for him or those moments in the middle of the day where—caught like a deer in the woods by a stray bullet—he would sit alone in the office washroom and find signs of his personal fears among the scrawled vulgar graffiti.

To say nothing of that recurring gargoyle face at a moment of falling asleep. This nightmarish visage even invaded daydreams at work, interfering with his ability to get the most basic of tasks completed on time.

During one late and lonely night of free-floating anxiety, Harold opened up his laptop and began a deeper hunt for information.

How had that comic connected to this secret society?

Had anyone ever written a thing about these people, the ones in the mask?

And what about the creator of all this?

What's his name again?

Harold began typing in the search engine:

faces comic strip cartoons funny pages

Up popped the name:

Walter Winsom.

8

THE CARTOONIST

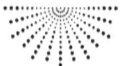

Harold clicked various links as a history of the father of *The Faces* began to build.

In the mid-1930s, this fellow named Walter Winsom, one of seven children in a midwestern farming family, hopped a train or three to Manhattan in hopes of making his fortune in the funny papers.

The young man apprenticed at the offices of various cartoon syndicates before launching early precursors to *The Faces*, including *Society Bloodhounds*, *Little Lola Lockup*, and *Scupperton Small'uns*.

Only one of these strips made it past the drawing board stage.

In *Little Lola Lockup* the storyline came from a real life saga of Verena Dolores "Lola" Brummage Lockeridge. This diminutive heiress to the Brummage & Spedwell Company's meat packing fortune survived Titanic as a child only to be arrested for the murder of her husband in 1936.

TITANIC TOT MURDERS MATE, read one headline.

But Lockeridge was far past tot status and into her thirties when she (allegedly) poisoned Ambrose "Skippy" Lockeridge, Junior, heir to the Lockeridge Hotel empire.

Winsom followed the trial's progress while writing frequent love letters to "Venomous Verena." He played a part in the surprising shift in public perception of Lockeridge through his series of very popular but controversial multi-panel strips.

Little Lola Lockup gave birth to a "Free Lola" movement, which—along with her wealth—could not have harmed the outcome of her trial.

Lockeridge herself certainly must've felt these "scribblings in the Sunday funnies" aided in her near-apotheosis. Soon after being acquitted, she sent an undisclosed sum to the young cartoonist with a note that stated, in effect:

Thanks, but go away now and leave me alone.

Although Verena's neck was saved, the comic strip was not. Winsom's syndicate cancelled a very popular *Little Lola Lockup* one week before Lock-

eridge's return to the welcoming ink of Knicker-
bocker's "Café Society" column.

Winsom, pushed out of his first major newspaper gig, possibly survived for a year off whatever
money Lockeridge had given him.

Still, it seemed that *Little Lola Lockup*'s minor
notoriety led directly to the mother strip to *The
Faces*.

Winsom had been sketching his fictional family
since childhood.

Some of the earliest versions showed up on
several collector sites after Winsom's death. Even in
these early attempts, one could see the births of
various Face family members.

These links led Harold to the first published
incarnations of this pleasantly unpleasant clan.

The rough, unsophisticated drawings barely resembled what would appear later.

These sketches and panels betrayed influences
from popular comics of Winsom's younger years,
including obvious homages to *Winnie Winkle*,
Smitty, and *Little Orphan Annie*. Each successive
attempt became tinged with a sense of perspective

that reminded one later critic of the German silent film *The Cabinet of Dr. Caligari* as well as the stylized ink-smitten caricatures of 19th century artist Aubrey Beardsley.

Winsom's next storyline launched in 1939, the same year that his parents and three younger siblings perished in a house fire, believed to have been started because his mother routinely smoked in bed.

This tragedy occurred almost a week to the day after Verena Delores "Lola" Brummage Lockeridge's deadly fall down the icy front steps of her Chicago mansion.

Winsom's new strip was called *The Pretenders*, a muddled but iconoclastic comic populated by a set of unusual characters whose faces changed week to week.

The masks appeared for the first time in this new creation.

The characters wore masks to cover their true faces, which were never fully depicted by Winsom.

The Face family were but one among several living in this small, bizarre community in the Midwest, a town surrounded by miles of cornfields and sunny skies, where unexplained house fires and other everyday tragedies barely fazed residents.

These townspeople tricked each other into believing they were just ordinary, nice people—despite the terrible traps they all set for neighbors and family members. There was not one iota of innocence, charm, or gentle humor to the strip.

In one episode, a teenaged girl lured her older sister into a broom closet and locked her in. No one ever let her out. In future strips, various characters might mention the noises coming from that closet, or the smell, or the fact that they still hadn't found the key—and hadn't someone left the only good broom in there?

"What a sad thing," said the old grandmother of the family as she looked outward from the newspaper to the reader. "Losing that broom."

In another story, a mother threatened to bake her young son into a pie if he didn't straighten up. This went on over the course of a few months while the kid kept causing trouble.

Finally, over dinner, her husband said, "Not sure why Dickie's missing his favorite dessert," to which his wife replied, "Who?" as she served a slice of pie and looked directly at the reader.

There'd be holes punched in a newlywed couples' canoe on the lake shore (to never return to dry land again), bear traps placed outside front doors, and local policemen who only arrested visitors to town "because you look like someone who might do something." A notorious paperboy delivered bad news while spreading dangerous gossip. A kindergarten teacher routinely led students into the high cornfields on field trips and left them there to find their own ways home.

Some never did. Parents didn't miss them.

Feuds were the order of the day.

Everyone in town wore the mask of nice.

Harold couldn't figure out why these funnies seemed so *funny*.

One modern writer—having studied the entire run of the strip—called it "a small town epic of cackling madness."

The Pretenders vanished from newspapers two years after its launch.

Winsom's career bounced back yet again just as America joined in the war. This time, he drew the least offensive group of characters from among *The Pretenders'* world:

The Face family.

In the newly-christened *The Faces* with its very first strip, Joe Face smiled and gave his famous, "Great day for a picnic" line as everyone around him wept and raged over the newspaper headline, "Pearl Harbor Attacked!"

Harold felt his excitement grow. How the hell did Winsom get away with this? Why would a newspaper syndicate allow this?

He found panels and strips full of racist and misogynistic jokes, a vigorous support of fascism, the McCarthyesque attitudes on display by the early 1950s, all within the context of the abusive ways this family dealt with each other and their neighbors, their lack of regard for basic kindness to others, the lying and stealing.

The cartoon family was full of horrible people doing horrible things.

And yet, somehow Winsom had gotten the tone right this round. One esteemed author of the time wrote this about *The Faces*, "Winsom knows what venom pumps through the dark heart of American life."

Harold wasn't sure if that author got it right. Walter Winsom was his own venom, and the dark heart seemed purely his.

But was the strip popular?

Oddly enough, it seemed to be — at least for a while.

By 1961, dropped by his syndicate, picked up by another, Winsom moved in a new direction.

The family went mainstream. Less caustic. A bit hip.

The boomer generation took to it as kids; even their parents loved following Joe Face's adventures. Storylines entered the territory of mild but quirky soap opera with a nearly *Howdy-Doody* twist. *The Faces* catchphrase seemed even funnier and sweeter when said by a seven year old: "Great day for a picnic."

Still, the Face family remained, at best, creepily benign. Harold became chilled by their metamorphosis as he scrolled on.

The family turned kinder in some ways, genuinely pleasant, unable to hurt a fly, with no interest in the usual mean jokes or horrifying moments.

To some extent, Harold felt he could sense the deterioration of Walter Winsom's mind in the forced inanity of this new version, the straitjacketed cousin of *The Pretenders*.

It wasn't more than a shade darker in intent than *Gasoline Alley* or even *Peanuts*, two of Harold's father's other favorite strips.

By 1971, the first generation of Face family Halloween masks hit the market. Children as young as seven or eight were in photos dressed up as various Faces.

A lost memory came back for Harold:

His father had given him a Joe Face mask when he'd been about nine years old. It was made of hard plastic with a thin elastic strap to hold it in place, very old-fashioned.

"Your grampa bought this for me," his dad had told him. "I used to wear it to breakfast just to shock your gramma."

His father told him all about *The Faces* then, showing Harold some books collecting the strips of the early '60s from their family library.

His father laughed as he read out their adventures.

Harold realized:

That was the moment.

That one Halloween, that one plastic mask.

It had not been his favorite mask. He could barely breathe beneath it, but his father liked it so much that little Harold wore it when they went trick 'r' treating together because it seemed important to his dad.

His father seemed happy on those days.

"What the hell?" he said, as he clicked the links back through the bizarre earlier incarnations to settle on the panel with the atomic bomb's mushroom cloud in the distance with the Face family in the foreground of a screaming crowd while Joe Face said, "Great day for a picnic."

How could past generations think of this as appropriate for kids to find in the newspaper?

What had been wrong with his *father?*

What was wrong with Walter Winsom?

Digging even deeper, Harold pulled up a news item from March 1985, a few years after Winsom ended the comic strip.

Walter Winsom was arrested for having set fire to his own home the previous Christmas. His wife and visiting adult children (and grandchildren) from Winsom's three marriages died that night.

Walter Winsom ended his days in prison, murdered by a cellmate.

Digging through every article with any mention of the subject, Harold found a photo of Walter Winsom late in life.

When arrested, police said he'd worn a Joe Face mask to hide behind.

But what hit Harold the hardest was Walter Winsom, unmasked.

His features were disfigured by scars, self-inflicted over many years.

It resembled the grotesqueries from Harold's nightmares.

He stumbled across other things, too, as he scrolled around. Photos of famous people, actors, politicians, moments of history, and in nearly every one, there was at least one *Face*.

Sometimes more than one.

9

THE JACKSON POLLOCK

S haring a sandwich at a restaurant near his office, Harold kept up a running critique with Margaret on passersby ("She needs a new look," she said, passing him a napkin, "doesn't she have any mirrors?" "You're terrible, but look at that couple to your left. Incestuous twins—or the most annoying lovebirds you've ever seen?") and somewhere in all that, a brief silence where Harold said, "It's weird about the cartoon."

"Why so obsessed with *that?*"

He didn't acknowledge her question. "This guy Winsom, absolutely nuts, with all the characters wearing masks and suddenly it's one of the most popular strips the '60s and '70s."

"I don't know what you find so interesting in all that stuff," she said. "I mean, come on. *Comic* strips?"

He thought a moment, reached for a few potato chips off her plate.

"Not much else going on right now, I guess."

"There's the you-and-me news," she said.

And there *was* news concerning the two of them.

The word "wedding" had been bandied about, lobbed, discussed, considered. First under the sheets, then on the carpet, in the back of the car, over a late breakfast in bed, once at a dinner out, twice among some of her colleagues—and then it became a thing.

It seemed perfectly natural that all elements of their future lives would fall into place. Despite wondering if it was the wisest thing in the world— this marriage business—Harold wore his two faces well.

The Harry face on the outside was nothing but thrilled with the upcoming nuptials.

"Well, that's old news now," he said, meaning the wedding, of course. "We should be asking what's the price of milk up to, and who's in the World Series this year. What should win an Oscar?"

"No idea," she said. "But I assume you heard

about what happened right next to our favorite old rendezvous?"

He had not.

"Well, according to what I saw on local news, some guy got beat within an inch of his life over there."

"*What?*"

"Right in the alley next to it."

"God. How awful."

"No kidding."

A moment of silence passed too quickly.

"Where we going to get a decent cup of cappuccino anymore?" she said.

"We can *still* go there."

"Not me," she said. "I'd wonder if some nutcase was sipping espresso while looking for his next victim."

Later, at home, Harold found the news piece in the paper.

Two photographs of the crime victim, both before the beating and after:

After, his face was a mess, unrecognizable as human.

The "before" picture showed an ordinary guy who happened to be a *Face*.

This didn't entirely surprise Harold.

He took the next day off from work and decided to drop by the favored haunt for a coffee and Danish.

He checked his phone—scanning emails, reading through a news article about some terrible incident elsewhere in the world, and glancing around at the few people sitting at tables or ordering at the register.

The entire time his mind was elsewhere.

He'd resisted going into the alley until he'd remained at his table a good ten minutes after finishing his little snack.

It was almost as if Harold counted the seconds one by one, waiting for a reasonable time to go to check the crime scene.

He listened to an internal *tick-tock* and wondered if anyone watched him, if another stalker might be sitting nearby *waiting to see if Harold would be ghoulish enough to walk outside and…*

Harold didn't hesitate a moment longer.

Stepping out into the cloud-dusted sunlight, he went along the sidewalk till he came to the gap between two buildings.

Harold felt a familiar shiver up the back of his neck.

While it wasn't an especially busy day down-town, there were plenty of people milling around. But no other Faces to be seen.

Harold stepped into the alley.

He'd expected police tape or even a chalk marking or some evidence of investigation, but because no one was murdered (as he told himself in the interior monologue of the moment) it likely wasn't so important a crime as to be further investigated.

But he did find something that looked odd, a smudge of something.

A smear on the wall?

He stepped in closer for a better view.

Specks and splotches where (he assumed) blood had sprayed out in all directions, Jackson Pollock style.

Even up the wall, a fountain of abstract art.

10

NAKED IN THE POOL

"Ugh. I wish I'd never mentioned it," Margaret said in the evening. "Why'd you even go there?"

Each of them leaned to their appointed sides of the queen-sized mattress while the little television screen on the wall showed some mindless garbage with the sound down.

"Just curious," he said.

"See anything?"

"Not really," he said. "It looked like nothing happened."

He wanted to make the Jackson Pollock joke, but it seemed too ugly and disturbing. He could predict that Margaret would accuse him of poor taste.

He remembered the phrase:

Cackling madness.

Margaret didn't need to know about that aspect of what Harold felt on the inside.

He'd begun to lie to her with some regularity.

This was a Harry thing, because you weren't supposed to tell the non-Faces much. And it wasn't even considered lying; you were protecting the "Non-Faced."

Life seemed so much safer being a Face—safer *and* more successfully lived. He became thrilled in an almost giggly and thrilling way when one of the other Faces spotted him somewhere—on the street, the bus, in his little junk heap of a car in traffic, at the movie theater.

They might nod or now and then say, "great day for a picnic," without any other words spoken.

Or he'd get the call from "Your brother Joe," for the occasional get-togethers where they all unmasked and relaxed over a few drinks.

He'd begun to look forward to those secret soirees.

During one of these parties—at a house so distant he wasn't sure his old car would make it—he showed up, had a drink, and they all ended up skinny-dipping in the kidney-shaped pool in back.

Glancing around he realized that unmasked none of them were particularly unattractive. With all their clothes off, they in fact were fine human specimens, the kind that should've been bedded and kissed and cared for, fed delicious meals, offered sumptuous wines, allowed to exist in paradise.

After drying off, he noticed a woman weeping in a corner by the row of narrow cypress just beyond the diving board.

Harold made his way over to her.

"You all right?"

Wiping her eyes, she glanced up.

"Allergies," she said. "Damn pollen."

He sat on the ottoman in front of her chair and drew out a tissue.

"Here you go. It's unused."

"You sure?"

"I keep crumpled ones in my right pocket and the pristine in my left."

"That's disturbingly hygienic." She wiped her eyes and then blew her nose. "Thanks."

"No need to return it."

"Was that meant to be funny?"

"Of course."

"I'm sorry, I'm not used to that."

"To what?"

"Humor." She straightened up, combing fingers through wet hair. "Haven't you noticed nobody's really funny at these things? Oh, they all think they are. But have you really listened to how people talk here? They like to mock everybody. Nobody's very nice."

Harold's first thought was: *but these are* our *people.*

"I hate these things," she said. "I'm Josie. Well, not really, but it's safer if you call me that."

"Harry," he said. "Sometimes Harold, but I'm switching to Harry for our kind I think."

"*Our kind.*" She didn't repeat the phrase as a compliment.

"If I upset you by coming over, I'm sorry."

"Don't be absurd," Josie said. "It's the damn Faces that upset me."

"I admit, it's a little weird."

"An understatement," she said. "You're still new. You'll figure it out eventually."

She began telling him of her "Journey In," as their kind called it. She'd experienced the usual feelings of isolation, things never working right for her, an inability to see a bright future all coupled with a general resentment and confusion over the way others played the game of life more successfully.

One "great picnic day" she met the mask or—as

club members called it in more metaphorical and mystical terms—"Embracing the Caul."

"Somehow it finds you, doesn't it? You're just minding your own business and then, maybe as a joke or for a party, *something*, you get this mask. This *cover*. You wear it once, and…well, you know the drill," she concluded. "It's really a cult. They just don't admit it. There's a secret language, a secret series of hand gestures and *of course* our own individual secrets."

"It doesn't seem *that* bad." Harold said this with a politeness that would no doubt have pleased Joe Face himself. "I mean, everyone seems to get along."

"They're afraid," she said.

"Of what?"

"Oh come on, admit it. We're *all* afraid. You could destroy me if you wanted to, you know, because of what I just said. But you won't, because I'd deny it and they trust me right now but they're still figuring you out."

"Nobody wants to *destroy* anybody."

"You'd be surprised. I've seen things."

"How long you been part of this?"

"Since I was seventeen." She must have read the look of shock on his face because she quickly added, "Yes, a mask-wearing member since high school. Don't ask why. Well, I'll tell you. I got in trouble with some people. I hated who I was. I was on a bad track."

"I guess we all were."

She changed the subject. "These parties get tiring at times. Have they given you the ground rules yet?"

"Sure," he said. "It's all hush-hush, you wear the mask in public at all times but can take it off at home so long as no non-*Face* is around. But..."

He hesitated.

She grinned for the first time. "You've done it, too. You take it off now and then. Maybe you find people who don't wear it and you take it off for them. Nobody talks about it here, but all of them do it. They just pretend they don't. Nobody's perfect. You know you're not even supposed to *sleep* with it off. And if you shower without wearing it, you have to make sure the bathroom door is locked to any outsider."

"I didn't realize any of that was very serious. I mean, who would wear it *all* the time?"

"Well, don't mention that to *this* crowd."

"Why not?"

She leaned forward and, in response, so did he until her mouth was as close to his left ear as she could get without licking it.

"You must've seen it in the papers. Or at least heard about it."

He didn't know what she meant, not at first.

Then, he did.

She nodded, as if reading the look in his eyes.

"Does anyone ever…" He hunted for the word he wanted to say, some euphemism to keep from reminding himself that this mask was more than it seemed.

"Escape?" she whispered. "I've heard one or two might have. But if so, they get far away from here. They stop communicating even with their oldest friends. They don't want anyone from the past to know where they end up. But…even then, who knows? There are a lot of us in the world."

He glanced across the pool to the lively party, the whole Face crowd, all of them laughing, telling jokes and sharing stories with each other.

"Yes, *them*," she said. "All these friendly people you've met here. They'll start following you. They probably already do. First, one of them pops up in the grocery line or on the sidewalk, maybe in places you go, your job, a restaurant. Then, others show up. You know what else? *You may not even notice they've got their masks on.* At least not till it's too late. They'll even seem friendly. Helpful. But if they even guess you've taken your face off…well, you may find yourself with broken bones and missing a few teeth in some dark alley. And that's if you're lucky."

She took a deep breath. "Truth is, it's not *always* a great day for a picnic."

11

THE NIGHT WEARS A FACE

Nocturnal wanderings became the norm for Harold.

He'd walk around the neighborhood, sometimes all the way to the local park and while arguing within himself, the two halves of who he was, and wondering what wearing the mask meant to both Harry and Harold, poor old insomniac Harold.

He couldn't shake the madness of Walter Winsom. Or a newspaper photo of his favorite movie star, noticing that even *he* was a Face. Or their state senator talking on the news—and he too had embraced the caul. The woman who owned the ice cream shop in town wore it. How could no one else really see this?

Other people, as well, although sometimes he couldn't quite tell for sure. He was almost *positive* they must've been wearing it, or they *should've* been wearing it, until this feeling became: *why aren't they wearing it?*

On the outside, everything was bright and wonderful and he should've been happy, but on the inside he knew anything that *seemed* good in his life was because of a rubber cartoon mask.

On endless nights, he drove out on the highway toward larger urban areas a couple of hours from his little city. He cruised wide boulevards, doing his best not to slow down when he noticed some night owl wandering alone beneath a halo of streetlights. Would this be yet another Face?

Do we ever stop finding our kind? he wondered. He'd have to ask at the next gathering. *Do we calm down inside? Can we sleep a full eight hours ever again? Will we worry that the mask might move or accidentally get pulled off?*

He drove aimlessly in the quiet of the dark until —exhausted—he headed back to his apartment for a few hours of oblivion.

Near the end of summer, he drove to the local park and sat in his car, feeling better there than lying next to Margaret or alone in his own bed.

He appreciated the sound of crickets and locusts, the stars through the trees, the silence of the neighborhood.

He awoke the next morning, still in the car, surprised he'd fallen asleep at all.

On his windshield, under the wiper, a parking ticket.

THIS IS NOT A TEST

After yawning and stretching, checking the time (*late for work, but no one will care, you're the golden boy at the job now*), he got out. Cursing his luck, he plucked the ticket from the wipers.

Not a ticket at all.

A note.

We should talk. I know you. I'll be here Saturday at three.

Harold was fairly sure the writer of that note meant three in the morning.

"Three in the morning" was always the special time. That hour existed as rite of passage as they adjusted to the life of the mask; the lonesome moment when they suffered through what the group called "The Great Change," after "The Journey In," when they began "Embacing the Caul."

Between work, dinners with Margaret, calling his parents about the wedding date they'd set, meeting with the realtor, and of course drinks with Whit and at least one of the Daves for Thursday Happy Hour, Harold began to feel a crushing fear about this note stuffed deep in his pocket.

Must be a trick. This is something terrible.

He thought of splashes of paint on a canvas and fountains of red.

Friday evening rolled in and out with Margaret, her mother and two uncles. Early Saturday morning, long before sunrise, he strolled around empty streets trying not to wonder about the note writer's intent but finding he could think of little else.

Harold stood at the south entrance to the park, near where he'd slept in his car earlier that week.

At an oak tree by a lamppost, someone stepped out from among the shadows.

Harold scanned the poorly lit park to see if any others were there.

He had an instinct to turn and run, but the man coming toward him began waving as he jogged over.

"Harold! It's me. It's okay. I just want to talk."

The sound of his voice broke the night's quiet. A dog barked from one of the houses nearby.

As the man approached, stepping directly into a pool of light, Harold recognized him.

"Remember me? I think it was your first party when we met. Out on Bloomington Road?"

"You've got to put it on, Bobby," Harold said, feeling protective. "There may be someone watching us."

"I'm pretty sure we're alone here." Bobby reached up to touch Harold's shoulder. "I knew you'd come."

Harold flinched and shrugged away from him. "Please put the mask on. Got it with you?"

Bobby nodded. He drew out a crumpled mask from his jacket pocket.

"Well, come on," Harold said.

"No," Bobby said. "It's all right. It's just us here."

"You don't know that," Harold said.

Is this a test? Are they checking to see if I'm loyal?

Harold glanced around. He was sure something moved in the shrubs over near the playground.

Harold felt his throat go dry. Goose bumps spread from his arms, past shoulders, up the base of his neck.

"What are you trying to pull here?"

"I've watched you," Bobby said. "You're different. You're not completely one of them. I can tell, Harold."

"It's Harry. And shut up. Just shut up, Bobby. Put your face back on. You're making me nervous. I don't like it. Is this a trick? Is this how you people gang up on those guys? The ones in the papers? The ones in the hospital? That woman who died?"

"Are you okay?"

"Shut up and put the mask on right now, Bobby."

"No," the man said. "And my name's Robin. Don't you want to stop this? I can tell you do. I see it in you. I've seen you drive around at night. I know the places you go."

"You *follow* me? You've been *stalking* me? Why? Have I broken some rule? What the *hell*."

"No, it's fine. Look, Harold…"

"Harry. I said it's *Harry*."

"No, you're *Harold*. This is just the two of us here. I know you. I've seen what you're going through. I've done all these things, too. And more."

Harold felt a wild heat rise in his face. He resisted the first impulse that came to him, which was to grab the guy's mask and just slap it over his face.

Calm down. Calm down.

It's a test, this is how they do it, those guys Whit and Dave and even that Josie character, they plant these things in your mind to test you. All those people lying in alleyways near death, they didn't pass it. They let a guy just like this trick them into giving up the mask and if you don't pass this, you fail and the only failure comes with broken bones and bloodied face and maybe they hound you to death afterward, who knows? They were unrelenting, these people, and there's no way to escape—and why can't Bobby just shut the hell up about all this?

"Please put it back on. Please put it back *on*," Harold kept repeating.

"What's the point, Harold?" Bobby began crying as he spoke. "What's the damn point?"

Harold took a deep breath. "Come on, buddy. The point is you're having a bad night, that's all. You have a good job. Everything is working out for you. Don't mess that up. Just put it back on and go home to your wife."

"She's one, too," Bobby said. "She never even takes it off in front of me. We've been married seven years and I never see her 'Face Naked.' We have two kids and I've never seen her actual face. You think you're nothing without the mask? We all think it eventually. That we can't handle things. Can't get good jobs. Can't have happy lives."

As Bobby spoke, his words flew by quickly and Harold felt as if he could barely breathe.

"You really happy like this, Harold? Is this life the one you really want? You feel people treat you like everyone else—only better? But you *know*. Inside, *all of us know*. We aren't like everyone else. We have to wear this rubber thing to convince them but sometimes I envy *any* guy who *never even found out* about Joe Face, who isn't first in line for promotions and doesn't have people falling off his every word just because he opened his mouth. I just want to be *me* again. Not this *Bobby*. Not Joe *Face*. You even look in *mirrors* anymore?"

Harold couldn't bring himself to answer. He felt heat rise under his skin. A kind of red hot lava in his brain. He glanced around, sure that there were others, sure that this was a trap that Bobby set up.

They trip you up. Our kind. It's a test.

"Why are you doing this to me?" Harold stepped closer, grabbing Bobby by the shoulders. "Stop doing this. Just *stop*."

Bobby cried out, pushing Harold away. ""Doing…what? I thought I could trust you. I've *seen* you before. I thought you were a good one."

"You want me to get in trouble, *that's* what you want. You think you're smarter than I am," Harry growled.

Harold didn't even recognize his own voice.

Every fear he'd ever had, the horrors of his dreams, the scarred face of Walter Winsom, the strange feeling he got in public—all of it burst out from his skin as he stood in the park talking to this dangerous man.

He glanced around, feeling sweat across his brow and dryness in his throat.

Harold saw someone else, a figure in the dark. He was positive.

It is *a trap. They're here.*

Bobby grabbed Harold by the collar and quickly drew his face close to his own.

"Don't do this, Harold. They want you to feel like this. It changes you. But don't do it. Just look at me. In the eyes. I'm not the enemy. I'm not what you should be afraid of."

But as these words spilled out of Bobby's mouth, Harold threw a punch to the other man's face and then another while Bobby's hands went up to defend himself.

Off-balance, they both went to the ground. Harold was sure his face would get bashed in and he'd end up in the hospital—or morgue—and he wasn't going to let that happen.

No way in hell, not because of this trap, a test.

Harold had a great job and a fiancée now. He made enough to buy a little house further out in better suburbs. This trick of *The Faces* wasn't going to destroy all that just because he happened to be wandering around with his thoughts before dawn.

Within him, Walter Winsom whispered about picnics while the rules of the Face game ran over and over again in a loop as fists rose and fell and *he* was doing it, *Harry not Harold*, because Harry knew this was an assassin sent against him, someone who wanted to take him down, maybe even threaten exposure and he'd lose everything he'd gained in the past year, all his hopes for a better life.

Afterward, with the sun's first glimmer beyond the trees, Harold saw the others.

The entire Face clan, it seemed.

JoBeth, Jolene, Joe-Bob, JoJo, all of them standing there.

I passed. I passed, you goddamn Faces!

But he said nothing.

Somewhere under his mask, Harold could not find his voice.

He heard Whit whisper to him as a hand went to his shoulder, "All right, Harry, we'll handle this. Let's get you home. It's okay, it really is. You did nothing wrong. No one blames you. That guy had it coming. He knew the rules. You're good. He'll be fine. We'll take care of it. Don't you worry. We'll see you later on. You get some rest."

When Harold awoke in bed several hours later, he wondered what had really happened the previous night.

He could only remember snatches of it, bits and pieces, and he wasn't completely sure it had actually happened until he saw the newspaper that afternoon.

THE RAZOR'S EDGE

They delayed the wedding till September because of Margaret's work schedule.

Harold's mother told him she and his aunt would make the down payment on their new home as a wedding gift. Margaret's parents paid in advance for the entire reception. Margaret found the wedding dress of her dreams. Various Faces were to be his ushers.

Whit agreed to be his best man.

A few weeks before the wedding, they moved into their new place, a three-bedroom Cape in a subdivision ten minutes closer to Margaret's office. They bought some furniture and her parents gave them various heirloom pieces, too. They decided to wait to paint the place until after the honeymoon, which would be delayed until Thanksgiving when they both could more easily take time off.

"But do we *really* need a honeymoon at all?" Margaret said, ever the practical one. "It's not like we don't know every inch of each other at this point. We could do something smart like invest that money. I mean, *all* this cash thrown away on a wedding. It's *crazy*, don't you think?"

The wedding day arrived and she was getting her dress ready to take over to the hall at her parents' church.

Harold stood in front of the bathroom mirror when she opened the door right at the precise moment before he meant to put his mask back on after shaving.

He froze, afraid of what she'd say. Would she notice?

She'd caught him *Face Naked*.

She'd be reminded of who lived beneath his outer skin. It wasn't a pleasant skin that covered him, but it was his own and he felt ashamed and embarrassed, humiliated even, but with a little razor cut of fury bleeding out as well. He hated her intensely for the intrusion into his private moment, and worried how she'd react.

All this in a second or two of watching her reflection in the bathroom mirror.

She stepped over and drew the mask back down around his chin, tucking it under, reaching up to draw the rather unkempt hair by his ears over the thinnest edge of the rubber.

She took a step back and adjusted it again as if it had gone on slightly crooked before.

"There we go," she said. "Look, Harry, there's one thing I need from you."

He held his breath, afraid of what horrible thing she might say. Did she want the truth? Would he have to tell her about the things he did? The nights without the mask? The meetings? The alley with blood spatter? The horrible moment at the edge of the park when he stood over Bobby, and for a split second saw what he'd done to the man's face?

"I need you to promise me something," Margaret said.

He exhaled, ready for the worst.

"Anything."

He meant it.

"You've got to promise that you'll never take it off again."

It took him a few seconds to respond.

"But...but doesn't it bother you?"

She looked at him curiously.

"This," he said, his fingers barely touching the edge of the mask.

She put her hands to his shoulders, turning him back toward the mirror.

He looked at his reflection: the pleasantness, the basic decency, the *great day for a picnic* aura.

"This is the man I fell in love with," she said. "Right there. Right in the mirror. Right in front of you."

He wanted to tell her everything. He wanted their marriage to not suffer from this festering wound hiding in plain sight, this shadow world no one noticed except the Faces themselves, laughing and sneering at those who unmasked themselves to invite their own dooms.

The terrible Faces, inescapable once they recognized that you were one of them, that you *belonged to them*.

"What about what's underneath?" He barely got the words out.

He felt the weight of a hundred stones on his chest, the conflicts of memory and dream, regret and fury, and a haunted sorrow he could no longer bear.

"Oh, you *silly* man. *No one* needs to know who you are down there. *Ever*. Not even me."

He gazed in the mirror at Joe Face, himself:

Harry, a haunter of late nights and alleys, dark places and long-shadowed twilights.

He observed the woman he'd marry in just a few hours, his best friend in the whole world, Margaret, standing right behind him with her chin on his shoulder as her own lovely face slipped down, just a little.

ACKNOWLEDGMENTS

I owe a debt of gratitude to *all* Patreon.com/DouglasClegg members who supported the writing of this story.

Special thanks to these people in particular:

Aaron Meyer

Astrid Zielinski

Brick Marlin

Edward Brock

Joseph Mulak

Julie Tansey

Matt Schwartz

Robin Bruner

Shrader Thomas

Larry Kinney

ABOUT THE AUTHOR

Douglas Clegg is the *New York Times* bestselling and award-winning author of *Neverland, The Priest of Blood, Afterlife,* and *The Hour Before Dark,* among many other novels, novellas and stories. His first collection, *The Nightmare Chronicles,* won both the Bram Stoker Award and the International Horror Guild Award. His work has been published by Simon & Schuster, Penguin/Berkley, Signet, Dorchester, Bantam Dell Doubleday, Cemetery Dance Publications, Subterranean Press, Alkemara Press and others.

A pioneer in the ebook world, his novel *Naomi* made international news when it was launched as the world's first ebook serial in early 1999 and was called "the first major work of fiction to originate in cyberspace" by *Publisher's Weekly,* covered in *Time* magazine, *Business Week, Business 2.0, BBC Radio, NPR, USA Today* and more. His book *Purity* was the first to be published via mobile phone in the US in early 2001.

He is married, and lives and writes along the coast of New England.

Find the Author Online:
www.DouglasClegg.com

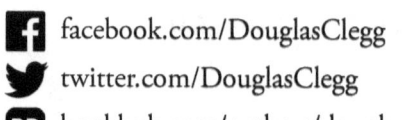

facebook.com/DouglasClegg
twitter.com/DouglasClegg
bookbub.com/authors/douglas-clegg